sleepover Girls

Sleepover Girls is published by Capstone Young Readers
A Capstone Imprint
1710 Roe Crest Drive
North Mankato, Minnesota 56003
www.capstoneyoungreaders.com

Copyright © 2015 by Capstone Young Readers

Library of Congress Cataloging-in-Publication Data is available
on the Library of Congress website.
ISBN: 978-1-4342-9758-7 (library binding)
ISBN: 978-1-62370-196-3 (paperback)
ISBN: 978-1-4342-9766-2 (eBook)

Summary: Ashley's got a passion for fashion, and she's always been the
most stylish girl in school — until the arrival of Sophie, a glamorous city
girl who's new at school. Sophie and Ashley are instantly inseparable,
but the other Sleepover Girls aren't so sure about Sophie. Things
get even worse when Sophie convinces Ashley to totally transform her
look. When Ashley includes Sophie in one of their weekly sleepovers, an
innocent spa party turns into a makeover gone horribly wrong.
Can Ashley get her groove back, or is it gone forever? And more
importantly, is Sophie worth all the trouble?

Designed by Tracy McCabe
Illustrated by Paula Franco

Printed in China by Nordica
0414/CA21400619
032014   008095NORDF14

sleepover Girls

The NEW Ashley

by Jen Jones

capstone
young readers

Maren Melissa Taylor

Maren is what you'd call "personality-plus" — sassy, bursting with energy, and always ready with a sharp one-liner. She dreams of becoming an actress or comedienne one day and moving to Hollywood to make it big. Not one to fuss over fashion, you'll often catch Maren wearing a hoodie over a sports tee and jeans. She is an only child, so she has adopted her friends as sisters.

Willow Marie Keys

Patient and kind, Willow is a wonderful confidante and friend. (Just ask her twin, Winston!) She is also a budding artist with creativity for miles. She will definitely own her own store one day, selling everything she makes. Growing up in a hippie-esque family, Willow acquired a Bohemian style that perfectly suits her flower child within.

Delaney Ann Brand

Delaney's smart and motivated — and she's always on the go! Whether she's volunteering at the animal shelter or helping Maren with her homework, you can always count on Delaney. You'll usually spot low-maintenance Delaney in a ponytail and jeans (and don't forget her special charm bracelet, with unique charms to symbolize each one of the Sleepover Girls). She is a great role model for her younger sister, Gigi.

Ashley Francesca Maggio

Ashley is the baby of a lively Italian family.
Her older siblings (Josie, Roman, Gino, and Matt)
have taught her a lot, including how to get
attention in such a big family, which Ashley has
become a pro at. This fashionista-turned-blogger
is on top of every style trend and shares it with
the world via her blog, Magstar. Vivacious and
mischievous, Ashley is rarely sighted without
her beloved "purse puppy," Coco.

chapter One

"Dunzo!" I exclaimed loudly. I proudly clicked the "publish" button on my laptop and watched the newest version of my blog appear on the screen. It felt like *forever* that I'd been trying to think of the perfect slogan, and at last, I'd finally gotten just the right burst of inspiration. The tagline on my blog now said *I put the 'Ash' in Fashion.*

"It just couldn't be more perfect!" I yelled, completely giddy with excitement.

"Library voice, please," joked my friend Maren in a nasal tone, after my outburst earned a few dirty looks toward our table. I clapped my hand over my mouth as if to apologize, but not before a little giggle escaped. Maren's impressions were always dead-on, whether they were of a cranky librarian or a quirky classmate.

Willow leaned over to get a better look at my latest blog makeover. "Totally groovy," she said in approval. "I love the glitter outline on the letters, and the slogan is *so* you. Awesome."

Not to brag, but it kind of was. The bubbly font at the top of the page reads Magstar, with my new tagline in swirly font right underneath it. Next to that was a selfie pic of me wearing star-shaped sunglasses and making the standard kiss face. In case you're wondering, the blog's name is inspired by my last name (Maggio), but coming up with a fun slogan to go with it had always stumped me. At last, everything was picture perfect!

"Aren't you supposed to be studying geography?" Delaney reminded me. "This test is going to be tough."

She had a point. Midterms were right around the corner, and I was the only one who didn't have my head buried in a book. Willow was doing pre-algebra problems, Delaney was reviewing the map of Africa, and Maren was reading her copy of *Where The Red Fern Grows*. I knew I should probably buckle down, too. But it was so much more fun to bling out my blog!

"I know, I know," I replied. "But who needs geography? After all, this new blog design could really put *me* on the 'map.'"

"Ba-da-bump!" laughed Maren. "And I thought I was supposed to be the funny one of our group."

Another annoyed *"Shhh!"* came from the other side of the room. I guess some people were actually at the library to study. As for us, it was nothing new to get shushed. When the four of us were together, things got loud. Come to think of it, my life was always loud. Between my friends and my big Italian family, silence was not a common occurrence in my world.

"Maybe it's time for a break," urged Maren impatiently. She was always seeking an excuse to do something other than sit down and read.

Maren didn't have to beg us to ditch the books for a bit. We decided to go get some fresh air on the lawn outside the library. As far as I was concerned, it didn't hurt that it just *happened* to have a great view of the baseball diamond where cute guys were always practicing.

But before I could get my baseball player fix, Maren noticed a flyer on the bulletin board in the lobby.

"Yes! she said excitedly, ripping it down for a better look. "They're already starting to promote the play."

We all crowded around Maren to see what the flyer said. "Take a trip down the rabbit hole at Valley View Middle School with our fall production of *Alice in Wonderland*," read the colorful piece of paper, which was shaped like the Mad Hatter's hat.

Maren put it on top of her head like she was wearing it. "What do you think? Do I have a shot at the part?" she asked, doing a little curtsy and making a funny face.

That was a no-brainer. "I'm no casting agent, but I'd book ya in a heartbeat," I told her. "You're practically president of the drama club, anyway. You've got this one in the bag!"

Maren's face brightened. "Thanks, chica," she said. "I'm kind of the underdog as a lowly sixth-grader, but I'm still gonna bring it."

"Whatever happens, we'll celebrate your audition at the sleepover on Friday," promised Delaney. "Can you say raspberry fizz slushies?"

Just thinking about Delaney's tasty slushies made me want to fast-forward to next weekend. The only thing that beat my blog on my list of "favorite things" was our sleepovers! They had become a tradition for us four and earned us the name the "Sleepover Girls" at school. Yep, from school to studying to sleepovers, the four of us were pretty much attached at the hip — and it was amazing.

Once we got outside, Delaney and I just wanted to lie down in the grass and veg out, but Maren was still all revved up. She seemed to have one foot in Wonderland already. "You guys *have* to get involved in the play with me," she insisted. "This isn't elementary school anymore! The production value will be way better, and so will the acting."

I couldn't help but smile at her mention of our elementary school plays. Maren had starred in pretty much *all* of them, and she'd always roped us into helping out behind-the-scenes. We'd all sworn we would "retire" after last year's disastrous production of *Snow White*, but it seemed like Maren wasn't going to let that happen.

Always the artist, Willow was the first to cave in. "I guess I could help out with the scenery and props," she offered. "I bet the tea party scene would be a blast to find stuff for! "

Maren nodded in approval. "Awesome," she said. "Those giant mushrooms aren't going to build themselves. What about you, Ash? I'm sure the costume department could use some of your fashion flair."

"Thanks, Mar. I'll think about it," I said, not wanting to commit. I already had a lot going on with all my blog stuff, and I also wanted to join the sewing club at school. I didn't want to overdo it.

Just as I was about to change the subject, I saw a complete fashionista walking out of the library. Her hair was slicked back Gwen Stefani-style, and she was wearing a black sweater dress with giant hoop earrings. Who was this girl? Valley View wasn't a very big town, and we knew most of the kids our age.

And then, as she got closer, I saw "it." There is no way that was what I thought it was. I had to check it out.

"Hey!" I yelled, getting up to sprint over to the girl. "Um, sorry to bother you," I said, out of breath. "But is that one of the new Sirena Simons bags?"

The girl looked surprised. "Oh, yeah, it is," she said, shifting the bag so I could get a better look. "Gorge, right?" That was an understatement! It was a quilted leather tote with tiny skulls-

and-crossbones inside each diamond; Sirena's style was definitely impossible to miss. But the million-dollar question was: how had this girl snagged it? Everyone online was buzzing about this purse, but no one could get one.

But before I could get the inside scoop, her mom honked the horn from the parking lot. "Let's go, Sophie," she called out the window, giving me an apologetic wave. "We need to get your library card and go pick your sister up at the stables."

The girl I now knew as "Sophie" gave me a thin smile. "See ya," she said, sauntering down the path. Wistfully, I watched the bag go with her. Why hadn't I thought to snag a quick photo for Magstar? Oh well. At least my designer radar had been on target.

chapter Two

Other than it raining like crazy, the next day at school started out just like any other day. Still a little soggy, Willow and I headed to homeroom together and took our seats. (Out of three groups, we were both in the "middle" homeroom since our last names were Keys and Maggio; Delaney and Maren weren't so lucky, since their last names were Brand and Taylor.)

Whichever one you were in, homeroom was pretty pointless — roll call, announcements, all the usual blah stuff. It was usually hard for me to stay awake, as I'm not much of a morning person.

When I saw Sophie walk into the room with our teacher, Ms. Duffy, I suddenly snapped back to life. I'd had no idea she was a new Valley View student!

Not surprisingly, she looked ridiculously chic. She was wearing a sheer sleeveless shirt over a black cami, and a studded belt topped off dark skinny jeans and black ankle boots. Her hair was up in a topknot, and her earrings were shaped like guitar picks. Total rock star.

"Meet your newest classmate, Sophie Hanlon," said Ms. Duffy. "Her family just moved to Valley View from southern California. Sophie, why don't you tell everyone a little bit about yourself?"

Sophie wrinkled her nose. She seemed kind of annoyed. Maybe she didn't like being in the spotlight? "Well, like you said, I'm originally from LA," she said, looking down. "My dad works for a record label. He got transferred here to Portland, so here I am."

Out of the corner of my eye, I saw Franny and Zoey, aka the "Prickly Pair," rolling their eyes at each other. The terrible twosome probably didn't like the thought of anyone new that could swoop in and take over their popularity throne. Identical twins, they'd earned their infamous nickname thanks to their mean girl ways, and more often than not, they gave new meaning to the words "double trouble." Needless to say, we really weren't friends. However, I have to admit that they can be nice sometimes, which is almost worse because you don't see it coming.

"Thanks, Sophie, and welcome," finished Ms. Duffy. "Let's all try to help Sophie get adjusted and catch her up on what's happening here at school. I'm sure you'll be in the swing of things in no time."

She showed Sophie to her seat, which happened to be just a few ahead of mine in the next row. I tried to make eye contact with her, but no luck. Instead, I exchanged glances with Willow, who seemed equally intrigued about this glamorous new girl.

I tried to listen as Ms. Duffy ran down the school happenings for the week, but I couldn't stop staring at Sophie (which probably seemed a little creepy). It wasn't everyday a new fashionista strolled into our small town. After class, I tried to catch up with her and say hi, but Delaney stopped me in the hallway before I could succeed.

"Yo, Maggio!" she greeted me cheerfully. "You ready for this social studies test?" I shook my head. I already knew this one was going to be a lost cause. "Not even a little bit," I admitted. "Where's Zambia again?"

She giggled. "Oh, you know, it's that one that's not Malawi or Mozambique," she joked. "Just use the process of elimination."

I covered my face with my leopard-print scarf. Most of the time, I was totally on top of my game when it came to schoolwork. But there had been way too many distractions lately. "I think I'm coming down with something," I said, forcing a fake cough.

"You'll live," said Delaney in her no-nonsense way, which was usually adorable but right now made me want to ship *her* off to Zambia.

As it turned out, luck was on my side. Mr. Costa announced that he would be moving the test to Friday to give us a few extra days to study. When does *that* ever happen? So I had a little spring in my step for the rest of the day — especially when I spotted Sophie in the caf at lunch. She was sitting at a table, eating an apple and reading a copy of *Elle* magazine. Since she was all by herself, that gave me the perfect "in" to introduce myself!

"So you're Sophie, huh?" I said, sitting down in front of her. "I didn't get a chance to introduce myself yesterday. I'm Ashley, also known as the weird fangirl from the library."

Sophie glanced up from her magazine and smiled. "Yeah, I was pretty impressed that you were able to spot a Sirena Simons, especially from far away," she said.

"Are you kidding me?" I told her. "That bag has more followers on Twitter than the president! I'd know it anywhere!"

Sophie gave me a curious look. "Funny, it doesn't seem like your style," she said, looking me up and down. I suddenly felt hopelessly uncool in my girly denim jumpsuit and scarf. She was kind of right, though. I wasn't really into all black clothing and skulls. However, a great purse was a great purse. (Just ask the dozens in my closet.)

"Oh, well, I follow all types of fashion," I explained. "I actually have a blog, Magstar, so that's how I keep up what's happening across the style spectrum." I'd heard someone use that phrase on one of the many fashion shows I watch not too long ago, so I thought I'd use it to try to sound cosmopolitan.

But it didn't work. Sophie seemed unimpressed. "No offense, but I'm surprised you can find anything to blog about around here," she sniffed. "The malls in LA were so much better. Now all I have is a postcard of Rodeo Drive."

The comment seemed a little snobby, but I guess coming from fashion designer central to tiny ol' Valley View *would* be a big adjustment. "I totally get it," I told her. "It's my goal to hit all the big fashion capitals someday. My dream would be to get a media pass and go to New York's fashion week!"

"You totally should. I went one year with my dad," Sophie replied, like it was no big deal. "He got me and my friend Jana second-row tickets to some of the coolest shows." She started telling me all about the big stars she'd spotted there. I was in complete shock. This girl was unreal!

It was all starting to add up — her dad, the record label, being from LA, Sophie's glam look. This girl had the best life ever! None of my friends had ever been to New York City before, let alone watch famous people rock the runway. But before I could ask her about what it's like to go to the top of the Empire State Building or shop at Bloomie's, Maren, Delaney, and Willow showed up at our table with their trays.

"We were about to put out a missing persons report!" exclaimed Maren, taking the seat next to me. She stole a French fry from my plate. "Luckily, Delaney spotted you over here. Who's the new girl?"

Could Maren be more rude? How embarrassing! I hadn't meant to ditch the girls for our daily lunch date. But before I could make the intro, Sophie stepped in. "I don't really have time to stick around," she said. "Gotta go fill out some paperwork before lunch period is over. Nice meeting you, Angela!" And with that, she slung her mesh tote over her shoulder and headed off without acknowledging my friends at all.

Delaney rolled her eyes. She had no patience for anything even remotely pretentious, and she also didn't like anything that broke up our little circle — even if it was only for part of lunch break. "What's *her* deal?" she asked. "Whoever she is, I guess she's tool cool for school. She couldn't even get your name right!"

Willow piped in, eager to ease the tension. "She's new here," she offered. "They introduced her this morning in our homeroom. Her name is Sophie."

"Well, she could have at least taken the time to learn our names," huffed Delaney.

Willow handed her a piece of licorice to lift her spirits. "Soon enough, I'm sure," she said, taking a bite of a kale chip. "I bet it's not easy being the new person at school when everyone is already friends with each other." Leave it to saintly Willow to play the peacemaker! She is such a sweetheart.

Maren shrugged, grabbing a piece of licorice for herself. "Yeah, maybe we could invite her to have lunch with us tomorrow," she offered. "Plus, we have way more important things to talk about — like the play! You're all coming to the info meeting after school, right? I can't imagine any of us would miss it."

The girls started talking about *Alice,* but I felt distracted. Sophie's life seemed so interesting, and it was hard to find other people that got as crazy as I did over fashion. I was pretty excited at the possibility of having a fab new friend! (That is, if she ever learned my name.)

chapter Three

The auditorium was packed when I walked in later that afternoon for play orientation. It was ridiculously loud as well, which I should have expected with that many excited teens in one place. Taking a look around the room filled with seventh and eighth graders, it was totally obvious that we were the new kids on the block. (Although actual "new kid" Sophie was nowhere to be seen.) Luckily, I spotted the other Sleepover Girls down in front and went to sit with them.

"Welcome to Wonderland!" the drama club moderator Miss Palladino greeted us, earning a crazy amount of cheering, chanting, and loud whistles.

"I wanna be the Dormouse!" yelled Kevin Smith over the craziness. That mental picture was kind of hilarious since he was the school's quarterback and about the least "mousy" person around. (Hmm, maybe this play thing would be a good way to meet some cute new older boys? I hadn't even thought of that until now! What a bonus!)

Miss Palladino just gave him a stern look and passed out the character breakdowns. She was clearly ready to get this play started and didn't want any distractions, even if Kevin Smith was the quarterback.

As she started talking, Delaney scribbled something in her notebook and put it in my lap. *It's official! Maren talked Willow and me into doing set dec. History repeats!* she'd written. *Are you gonna play wardrobe stylist?*

I felt a little annoyed. I'd come to the meeting as a favor to Maren, but I'd never actually said I was going to help out with the play. Cute actors or not, part of me wanted to learn more about the time commitment before saying yes. I had a lot going on and wasn't sure I had any extra time to put into the play. Plus, I barely had enough time for my blog as it is. Did I really have time for this on top of everything else?

But would I ever let Maren (or any of the Sleepover Girls) down? Not a chance. So with a big sigh and a frown, I reluctantly wrote back, *Yeah, that's the plan.*

Once we split into committees, I joined the six other peeps who wanted to do wardrobe.

Among them were Sissy, a petite seventh-grader with a really high voice; Max, a super-tall eighth-grader who'd worked on every play since he started at VVMS; and Zoey, aka one-half of the Prickly Pair. (Oh, joy.)

I kind of tuned out as Zoey snapped into bossy mode and started talking about her vision for the perfect blue dress "Alice" should wear. Thankfully, soon I was saved from her endless droning by an unexpected visitor.

"*Angela!*" came a loud whisper from the doorway. I didn't pay it much attention until I heard it again. "*Angela!*"

I looked up from my notebook to see Sophie peering around the corner. She motioned to me to come join her. "Excuse me for a sec," I told the group, surprised. Most of them didn't seem to notice — they were too busy debating the merits of top hats. Really? I had no idea top hats were that important.

I tiptoed over to join Sophie in the hallway. "Oh, um, hey," I said, trying to act casual. Why did being around Sophie make me nervous? Maybe because she was so effortlessly cool. "What's up?"

Sophie flashed what looked like a credit card. "I was about to head over to the mall and wanted to see if you wanted to join," she said. "I'm in the mood to shop, even if the stores here are terrible." She waved the card in the air with a small smile.

Hmm, let's see: talk about top hats with Zoey or shop with a fellow fashion addict? Now *that* was a no-brainer.

"In," I told her. "Oh, and FYI? My name is Ash-ley." I grinned to let her know that I didn't mind her messing up my moniker.

She looked a little sheepish. "Got it," she said. "Name duly noted. I guess I should know my shopping buddy's name, huh?"

"It's a must," I told her, linking my arm through hers like we were already good friends. I was feeling less intimidated by the minute. "Plus, you need someone to show you that the Valley View mall isn't *that* bad."

I was about to head off without looking back, but Maren spotted us leaving "You're leaving?" she said, shooting a sideways look at Sophie. "We're just getting started!"

"They're not even going to notice I'm gone," I told her. "Promise. And I'll definitely come to the next meeting. Deal?"

"Well, where are you going?" asked Maren, crossing her arms. She wasn't letting me off that easy. Maren could be really tough (and almost scary) when she wanted to be!

Sophie stepped in. "Anywhere but here," she answered. "No offense, Mary. Let's go, Ash." She started off down the hall, and I shot Maren an apologetic look as I followed close behind. I wasn't sure if I'd handled that so great, but how many times do you get the chance to hit the racks with a runway expert? Around here, not too many!

After we'd hit three stores at the mall and were still going strong, I knew my choice had been the right one. So fun! "Oooh, let's go to Mayfair," I told her, steering us toward the escalator. "They've always got awesome deals."

The girls and I loved rifling through the bargain bins there and finding cute stuff for cheap, but I wouldn't necessarily call them "power shoppers." It felt good to have a new friend who was as fashion-obsessed as I was!

Not to take anything away from my three BFFs, whom my life would be incomplete without. But none of them really cared about clothes. Maren was a total tomboy, fearless and utterly hilarious — to her, the whole world was a stage. Calm and kind, Willow was everyone's favorite hippie chick, and an awesome artist. And smart, motivated Delaney was constantly taking on a new passion project — whether it be adopting a dog or starting an organic garden. I would never trade any of them for anything, but it was fun to finally have a sister in style!

Sophie wasn't so interested in our favorite spot. "Everyone wears that stuff," she said. "Let's go to Nordstrom instead. I want to check out the new line of Vivienne Westwood sunnies."

Though I was a little bummed to skip Mayfair, I was always down to do the department store thing (even though everything was super expensive and I usually couldn't buy anything). But, as it turned out, Sophie was a *pro!* After we snapped a few pics of the new Vivienne Westwood sunglasses (which were crazy amazing) for my blog, we waltzed through all the different departments, admiring sky-high stilettos and sequined sheaths. Even if I couldn't afford most of the stuff, it was a blast to roam through the racks. I felt like I was shopping with a celebrity!

"So what's this play all about?" Sophie asked, holding up a lacy black sweater to herself in front of the mirror. "I used to do theatre stuff at my old school, except our plays were in French. I've never done a normal play before."

French? This girl was getting more sophisticated by the minute. When she saw my confused look, she explained, "I went to a private school in LA called Lycee Francais where they teach both languages. It was THE school if you wanted to be someone."

"*Tres chic*!" I replied, impressed. (And glad I knew, like, two French phrases — that being one of them.) "Forget New York, then! Let's go to Fashion Week in Paris sometime instead."

If we ever *did* make it to Paris, it was becoming clear that Sophie would make the most of it shopping-wise. The girl was on a roll — even I was having a hard time keeping up!

Once we hit the juniors department, she tried on pretty much everything she set her sights on. We snagged a giant dressing room, where I filled her in on all things *Alice* and the other school gossip. I even made her laugh with my story about how Franny and Zoey had brought a caviar spoon to show-and-tell once. And once she'd finally worn out her options, she began playing personal shopper for me, much to my delight!

"You *have* to try this on," she said, handing me a black tulle skirt with little red rosebuds on it. "It's like the perfect combo of girly-meets-goth, which could be your new look."

I hadn't realized I needed a new look, but Sophie clearly knew what she was doing. Looking it over, it definitely wasn't my usual style, which I would probably describe as classic, cute, and colorful. But if Sophie thought it would work, I had to try it. "Ooh, and it's on sale for $30! But unfortunately I still can't afford it. Just call me your window-shopping wing woman," I said.

"No biggie," Sophie shrugged. "If it fits, I'll buy it for you. You can thank my little plastic friend!" She waved the card in the air again.

"Your dad just *gives* you his credit card to use?" I asked, totally in awe. Sounds like Sophie had won the parental jackpot! I was lucky if my allowance allowed me to buy a pair of earrings at Charming Charlie's once in a while.

Sophie laughed. "It's a pre-paid debit card," she explained. "He just loads it up and then I can spend it however I'd like. Which, as you can see, as on clothes — and new friends."

By the time we made it up to the cash register, Sophie's stack of clothes had grown so big that I could barely see her underneath it! It was like a movie!

So this is how the rich and fabulous live, I thought. Maybe I should change my career goal of fashion designer to record producer? She laid the pile on the counter and snatched my skirt out of my hand. "Seriously, this one's on me," she said. "Consider it an apology, 'Angela.'"

She handed the card to the cashier to run through the processing machine. "This card only has $39 on it, but your total is $342," said the cashier. "Do you want to come back with one of your parents?"

Sophie wrinkled her nose, irritated. "No," she said, frowning. "My dad must not have re-loaded it this month. Here, we'll just take this one for now." She handed the cashier the tulle skirt.

All those cute clothes she'd picked out, and she was going to get *me* something instead? "No way!" I exclaimed, embarrassed that she would do that for me. Sophie shook her head.

"It's no biggie," she said. "I'll just have my dad's assistant come pick up the rest of the stuff later this week."

I was totally taken aback. Sophie wasn't a snob — in fact, she was kind of selfless. "Thanks, California girl," I told her. "I totally owe you one."

"Just wear it to school tomorrow," she said. "Seeing you rocking that skirt is all the thanks I need!"

I put the skirt in front of me and did a little ballerina twirl. "Done and done."

chapter Four

The next day, Sophie met me in the bathroom before school to get a sneak peek of *the* skirt. I'd paired it with a black lace top and red lace-up ballerina flats, which Sophie seemed to like. She herself was clad in a black V-neck and jeans, topped off with a black hipster hat. "Well, hello, Black Swan," she said, whipping out her fancy makeup bag. "Now all you need is the perfect cat eye and red lip."

I didn't usually wear such bold make-up, but I didn't want Sophie to think I wasn't sophisticated. A few master strokes later by Sophie, and my updated look was complete.

"*C'est magnifique!*" Sophie said, putting her makeup bag back. "Homeroom won't know what hit 'em."

Oh no! Homeroom! I looked at my watch: 7:59. Just one minute to get there! Poor Willow had probably been waiting for me in the usual spot, wondering where I was.

"Let's go," I said. "Ms. Duffy makes you stay after school if you're late."

"I'm not too worried," said Sophie, putting some pink lipstick on herself. "But I'll follow your lead."

When we walked in just as the bell rang, we both dissolved in laughter. I felt a little guilty when I caught Willow staring at us, so I gave her a little wave and mouthed "Sorry" after I sat down in my seat. Hopefully we could all eat lunch together and the girls could get to know Sophie, too.

Sounds like a great plan, right? But unfortunately, it didn't quite turn out as I'd hoped (which is always a bummer).

The trouble started when I was waiting in the lunch line for some lemon chicken and veggies. Maren came up behind me with her tray and wasted no time commenting on my outfit. "Um, are you going to a funeral or something?" she asked. "You never, ever wear black."

I had to admit, she was kind of right. "Oh, you know me, always trying to set a new trend," I replied. "Plus, every girl needs to try something new once in awhile."

"Yeah, but does every girl need a little black tutu?" she laughed. "That one looks like it came straight out of the drama club's costume closet, which isn't a good thing."

Ouch! That was a bit harsh, even for straight-shooting Maren. I decided not to tell her Sophie had picked out the outfit, especially since she was already made about me ditching out of the play meeting.

Instead, we grabbed some food and headed back to the table, where Willow and Delaney were debating which member of our fave boy band was the cutest. It was an argument that I found kind of refreshing, since I was usually the only one who crushed on boys. I was about to chime in with my two cents when I spotted Sophie coming through the cafeteria doors.

"Sophie!" I called, waving her over to join us.

She headed our way, toting a retro Hello Kitty lunchbox. Too cute! Sophie seriously had the best style. But before I could compliment her on it, Willow piped in to pick her brain. "Quick! Who's the hottest one in Fyve Fellas — the cutest boy band of all time?"

"Who knows? I stopped listening to them in third grade," she replied.

Delaney's eyes narrowed. It was time to diffuse the tension. "Well, I think Brad is the cutest," I cut in. "Btw, Sophie, *love* the lunchbox."

"Thanks! I collect Hello Kitty stuff, so I couldn't resist when I saw it at the vintage shop," she said, popping it open to reveal its contents. "Anyone want some fruit and nut quinoa?"

"Quin-*huh*?" said Maren. "Never heard of it."

Ever the health nut, Willow chimed in. "It's kind of like rice, but healthier," she explained. "I love it!" She took a spoonful, giving an enthusiastic "mmm" for emphasis. "I'm Willow, by the way. We're in the same homeroom."

I snapped to attention. "Oh, yeah, you haven't even officially met everyone yet! This is Willow, Delaney, and Maren," I told Sophie. "Everyone, this is Sophie."

"And you're from LA, right?" asked Maren.

At Sophie's nod, Maren replied, "That's really cool! Do you know any famous actors?" Leave it to Maren to ask that question, as she hoped to be an actress someday. I appreciated her including Sophie in the conversation.

"There were a few that went to my school," Sophie answered, as if it was no big deal. "Shira Clay was in my class at Lycee Francais."

We were all obsessed with her show, "Suddenly Shira" — Delaney, especially. But Delaney didn't freak out the way I thought she would.

"Oh, that's cool," she said flatly. "We've met some celebs here in Portland, too. Maren, tell Sophie how you got to hang with Luke Lewis."

Was it my imagination, or did Delaney seem like she was being competitive with Sophie? That was unlike her.

"Oh, yeah, it was pretty awesome," Maren said, drawing a happy face with ketchup on her plate. "It's kind of a long story, but we went all-out for this radio contest and made this crazy scrapbook about Valley View. We didn't even win, but I still got to meet him in the end!"

Sophie seemed a bit bored. "That must have been exciting to meet a celeb here in Valley View," she remarked. "Living in LA, it would have been no big deal. Maybe I can talk to my dad to see if he can sign Luke to the record label he's starting."

That was weird. I thought Sophie had said her dad had been transferred by his company, not starting a new one. I realized that even though we'd been hanging out, I really didn't know much about her or her fam yet.

"That would be awesome!" I told her, trying to ignore the "looks" Delaney and Maren were giving each other. "Your family sounds so glamorous. Do you have any siblings or anything?"

"I do have an older sister, Trina," shared Sophie. "She's a sophomore at the high school."

"Oh right, I remember your mom mentioning something about picking her up at the stables the other day," I recalled. "Does she have her own horse?"

At Sophie's nod, Willow looked impressed. "I've *always* wanted a horse," she admitted. "Maybe your sister could give me a lesson at the stable some time. What's her horse's name?"

Sophie looked uncomfortable. "Oh, I don't remember," she said. "Probably something cheesy like 'Flicka' or something. She's a total book nerd."

"*My Friend Flicka* is actually a pretty good book," said Delaney, twirling some pasta around her fork. "Oh wait, you probably only read *Teen Vogue*."

Okay, now I knew it wasn't in my imagination. Delaney was *not* digging Sophie. And it seemed that the feeling was starting to be mutual, based on Sophie's response. "I'm glad you know me so well after one day," sniffed Sophie. "Actually, I read all the time. I just finished *Crime and Punishment* this summer while my family was traveling through Europe."

"Well la-di-da," said Delaney quietly, under her breath.

"And let me guess, you only listen to world music, too," chimed in Maren. "After all, it's *so* immature to listen to stuff like Fyve Fellas and Luke Lewis."

This was turning into a sinking ship quickly! And it didn't help that Delaney and Maren were rocking the boat. I needed to do something to turn it around and show the girls why Sophie was worth giving a chance. Otherwise, I might have to say *sayonara* to my new friend. Or even worse, I would have to say goodbye to my old friends!

chapter Five

Should I or shouldn't I? You know what they say: "If you don't explore, you'll never discover." But my sister Mathilda always says, "Look before you leap."

It felt like the 400th time I was hearing Alice's monologue, and at this point, I knew it by heart. Delaney, Willow, and I were sitting in the auditorium waiting for Maren to take her turn onstage, but it was taking forever and a day to get through the play tryouts.

To pass the time, Willow was sketching something in her notebook, and Delaney and I were scrolling through random Instagram feeds on her iPad. *Our* hashtag right now? #totallybored.

As if things couldn't get worse, the next person up was Franny. I guess if she got the part, she'd have an automatic look-alike understudy! Just one of the many benefits of having a twin, I imagine.

But, as it turned out, our class' resident drama queen may have had *too* much of a flair for drama. She was practically yelling the lines, and her gestures were over the top. It was kind of like a "what not to do" tutorial for actresses. It was a little surprising and a lot funny.

"Is this ever going to end? I'm late for a very important date," Delaney whispered, and we both stifled our giggles so no one could hear. It felt good to laugh together. I guess she wasn't mad at me for the whole Sophie thing yesterday. We watched as Franny strutted offstage, oblivious to the fact that her audition had bombed. To the rest of us, it seemed obvious that she'd be joining her sis Zoey on our costume committee rather than taking the stage as the lead.

Mercifully, Miss Palladino took the stage a few "Alice" hopefuls later and announced that it was time for the Mad Hatters to have their shot.

"Go Maren!" Delaney yelled loudly, as we watched Maren file onstage with all the other would-be Hatters. Out of fourteen people trying out for that role, she was one of just a few sixth-graders and the *only* girl. (That was our brave and confident Maren!) There is no way you could get me to do that!

Kevin Smith was up first; apparently, he'd changed his mind about becoming the

Dormouse. Loud and goofy, he seemed like he'd make a pretty good Mad Hatter. (Although it would be a shame to cover up that cute face with a bunch of makeup!) But I knew Maren would give him a run for his money, and I was right.

"Greetings all, let me introduce myself," she said, tipping an imaginary top hat. "I'm Tarrant Hightopp, better known as the Mad Hatter." She did a little tap dance, getting a laugh from everyone sitting out in the audience. Then she launched into her Mad Hatter monologue:

Twinkle, Twinkle, Little Bat,
How I wonder what you're at.
Up above the world you fly
Like a tea tray in the sky,
Up above the world you fly
Like a tea tray in the sky.

As soon as she was finished, we all burst into applause. She definitely had a fighting chance at landing the role. Maren threw a little thumbs up sign our way, then sat back down to join the other candidates with a big grin on her face. She nailed it! I was so proud of her, and I could tell my other friends were as well.

Miss Palladino was getting ready to move onto the Cheshire Cat tryouts when someone rushed down the aisle past us.

"Am I too late?" asked Sophie, who looked every bit the part in a tall top hat, velvety coat, and striped pants. Say *what?* She hadn't mentioned she was interested in the play. She made it seem like this play wasn't quite up to her standards, and now she was trying out? I squirmed in my seat uncomfortably. Maren was *not* going to be happy about this.

"You're just in time," said Miss Palladino, making some notes. "Go for it."

Sophie took the stage, and all her theatre experience shined right through. She was totally confident and captivating — with just the right amount of quirkiness for the Hatter. She was amazing.

I felt excited for her, but a bit worried at the same time. Who was I supposed to root for? Seeing the look on Delaney's face, I kind of wished I could drink a potion and shrink right now, as it seemed like the only way out of this mess.

Luckily, Maren didn't seem to be all that worried about her new competitor. After the tryouts wrapped, she came bounding over to us. "That took forever, but we *finally* made it through the looking glass!" she joked. "You guys rock for coming to support me. You are the best friends ever!"

Delaney put her arm around Maren protectively. "Are you kidding me? Of course," she said. "And you know we'll be front and center for the actual play, too."

Maren shivered with excitement. "I don't think I can wait a whole day to find out if I got it! I'm so happy tomorrow is only a half day," she said. "Will you guys come check the list with me tomorrow after lunch?"

"Not only that, but why don't we start our sleepover early and watch *Alice in Wonderland* right after?" Delaney offered. "My mom can pick up some cupcakes from that cute new place on Main Street, and we can brainstorm some fun ideas for props and scenery. Deal?"

"Deal," we echoed. If there was one thing the Sleepover Girls did well, it was stick together when one of us needed something! Nothing is better than a good group of friends, right?

Glancing toward the stage, I noticed Sophie chatting with Miss Palladino and a few of the other kids. And then, it hit me.

"Oh no! I completely forgot! I can't come early tomorrow. Sophie's letting me do a photoshoot with her Sirena Simons bag. I would cancel, but this could mean major traffic for my blog. You guys understand, right?"

Maren and Delaney exchanged a look. "Oh, okay," Maren said. She seemed disappointed. For once, she didn't have a wisecrack or one-liner, which made me feel every worse.

"Let me get this straight. You are skipping our sleepover tomorrow night to take a picture of a bag?" Delaney said with a look of annoyance on her face. She was clearly not happy about this and wasn't going to hide it.

"Of course not!" I said. "I'm just coming late, that's all." As if I would ever miss our Friday tradition.

But Maren didn't seem so sure of my loyalty. "Were you going to tell us or just flake out?" she asked.

Thankfully Willow jumped in and saved me from this attack. "Calm down, guys. We have a half day, so Ashley has plenty of time to do both things," Willow said.

I appreciated the help from Willow, but it didn't erase the looks I was getting from my so-called friends. Was it so wrong to have a new friend?

chapter Six

When I woke up Friday morning, four little
letters came to mind: TGIF! It had been an
eventful week, midterms were almost over, and
I was so ready for a fun weekend. With Sophie's
help, I'd already planned my outfit for today: a
lacy black shirt paired with a leather-looking
black skirt, and Converse sneakers to add a
little hipster flair. (Goodbye, pastels and bright

colors . . . hello, all black! Who was I again?) As I put it on, I couldn't help but remember the mini-fight I'd had with Delaney and Maren the day before about me hanging out with Ashley. This was the first time I wasn't completely pumped to go to a sleepover.

But first I had to make it through the day, which was sure to fly by since it was only a half day. Thank goodness for early release days! (At least midterms had one happy side effect.) Now the task at hand was to ace my geography test (where's Zambia again?) and keep Maren at bay until the cast list reveal after lunch. Having ADHD meant she was almost always antsy at school anyway, but today would definitely take the cake!

Once Mr. Costa passed out the geography tests, I knew I was in for it. My brain went to mush as soon as I looked at the map, and suddenly I was unable to distinguish Niger from Nigeria or Ethiopia from Egypt. I guess that's what I got for staying up late writing blog posts about black being the new black (a topic Sophie had suggested!).

The weirdness continued when I walked to lunch with Sophie. She informed me that she'd be taking Franny and Zoey up on their invitation to sit with them instead.

"Sorry, girl, but I felt about as welcome at your table as a Kmart shirt in a Chanel store yesterday," she said. I couldn't help but giggle at her joke, even though I was bummed that she wasn't going to sit with us again. "Plus, I'm probably even *less* popular with your friends now that Maren and I both tried out for the part of Mad Hatter."

I wanted to ask why she'd decided to do that, especially if she was trying to be friends with the Sleepover Girls. Maybe she didn't care? It was probably better to leave it be for now, as

I couldn't take much more drama. And also probably best *not* to let her know that we call Franny and Zoey the "Prickly Pair" (for good reason). Some things are better discovered for yourself.

And that's exactly what I told myself as I went to check the cast lists after lunch, a bit nervous about who was going to win the role. Of course, Maren was my first pick, being that she's one of my besties and all. But Sophie had totally rocked the audition, and it would be a great way for her to make new friends. So, I'm going the neutral route. May the best Hatter win!

Outside Miss Palladino's office, everyone was crowded tight around the bulletin board, making it hard to get close enough to actually see what the list said. Maren and Willow were stuck near the back of the group, trying to edge closer to the board. "Ash," Maren called, waving me over. "Got a pair of binoculars? I'm dying to see what it says!" She jumped up and down to prove her point.

But before I could respond, Franny and Zoey busted out of the pack, clearly smug with the knowledge of who'd landed what part. "Looks like you'll be enjoying the view from the wings with me, Maren," huffed Franny.

"Huh?" she asked, but Franny and Zoey just kept going. Maren pushed her way to the front of the crowd, running out of patience. When she came back to us, she looked devastated. "I got understudy . . . to Sophie. *She's* the Mad Hatter."

I felt awful. Maren had starred in every play in elementary school, and she dreamed of seeing her name in lights. Now she was going to be stuck behind the scenes instead of getting a chance to prove herself at our new school. It was then that Delaney showed up, out of breath from rushing to meet us.

"Well?" she asked, her eyes curious. Maren's frowny face told her everything she needed to know, and she immediately gave Maren a bear hug. "You'll get 'em in the spring," said Delaney in encouragement. "Was it . . . ?" The word "Sophie" hung heavy in the air.

I wanted to tell them how she'd bought me the skirt. How maybe she was just trying to fit in and meet new people. How it wasn't her fault that Miss Palladino had picked her to play the Mad Hatter. But I didn't get a chance, because as if on cue, Sophie strolled up to check the list.

"Eeee!" she squealed, when she saw her name in bold. Maren looked like she'd just heard nails on a chalkboard.

"Ash! I got it!" she yelled as she gave me a huge hug. "I'm so glad you told me about the play that day when we went shopping."

Delaney's face darkened again. "Well, at least she knows your name now," she muttered.

She turned her back to me, facing just Maren and Willow. "You guys still up for some cupcakes? I'm ready to get out of here."

"Yeah, I could use some icing on the crappy cake of today," replied Maren, her eyes narrowing toward Sophie. "Have fun at your photo shoot, Ash." Except she didn't sound like she meant it.

They headed off as a trio, with Willow throwing me an apologetic look over her shoulder as they walked away. Where was that rabbit hole again? Suddenly, I felt like disappearing down it.

chapter Seven

Sophie proudly perched the Sirena Simons bag in front of the white backdrop I'd set up. "Your muse awaits, madam," she said, motioning to my digital camera with a grin. She'd been in a great mood ever since we left school. How could she not? She had only been here a few weeks and was already the lead in the school play.

I should have been on cloud nine having the chance to shoot the bag for my blog, but I just felt down. "Sophie, can I ask you something?" I asked, eager to get it out of my system.

"Ask away," she said, tinkering with my tripod to move it into a better position.

I took a deep breath. "Why did you go for the part of the Mad Hatter?" I asked. "I mean, we talked about the play when we went shopping, and I told you how excited Maren was about it. Then you showed up out of nowhere at tryouts, and it kind of felt like you stole her role." I hoped I hadn't gone too far, but I felt the need to stick up for Maren.

Sophie looked annoyed. "I barely know Maren," she said.

"I know," I said, equally annoyed. "It just seemed like you didn't care since it wasn't as sophisticated as your French plays you did at your old school."

"That is not true. I thought the play sounded cool when you told me about it, and I already had the Mad Hatter costume. I thought it would be fun to get involved in theatre again, even if it wasn't in French. Does that make me an awful person?"

"No, totally not," I assured her, less annoyed after hearing her explanation. "I don't even know where that came from. I guess I just really want for you to be friends with my friends, and that felt like a step backward." It was like my mom always said — honesty really was the best policy. It felt good to let it out!

Sophie shrugged, taking a sip of her sparkling water. "I'm totally open to being friends with your friends," said Sophie. "But it kind of seems like the feeling isn't mutual."

I racked my brain for a solution. "I think we got off on the wrong foot. They're usually not like that, I swear, " I told her. "You should see how much fun we have at our sleepovers!" And then, my light bulb moment struck.

"That's *it!*" I exclaimed. "I think a sleepover would be the perfect way for everyone to really get to know each other. We can do one next weekend, with spa treatments, scary movies, the whole nine yards! I'm sure my parents won't mind."

"Count me in," said Sophie. "Consider it a clean slate on my end. And you know what? Don't worry about asking your parents. I'll host. It will be nice to have everyone over."

I was so relieved that Sophie was going to give my friends a second shot. Who says five's a crowd? Now I could concentrate on the fun part: shooting Sophie's bag. Ready to lighten the mood, I whipped out the camera and started snapping away.

"Oh, yeah, work it, own it," I joked, pretending like the bag was an actual model.

Sophie took my cue and picked up the bag, whirling around with it and kicking up her leg like she was a catalogue model. "I love that! Much better to have a person in the photo — makes it more lively," I realized, continuing to take lots of pics.

I turned on some music while Sophie played perfectly to the camera, dancing around and showcasing her handbag.

After we'd gotten a bunch of great photos, Sophie seemed inspired. "You never feature *yourself* on your blog," she said. "Why don't we pick some fab outfits out and we can do a selfie shoot?"

"Why not?" I answered. When she saw I was up for it, Sophie wasted no time rifling through my entire closet. Looking at the clothes she'd picked, I couldn't help but laugh. "You managed to find, like, the *only* black stuff in my closet," I told her. "You must have special radar!"

"I'll get you to the dark side yet," joked Sophie, tapping her fingers together like a cartoon villain. "Now get to posing, girlfriend. People need to see how amazing we are!"

As soon as she left, I dove into writing up the blog post about the Sirena Simons bag and doing a slide show of my "selfies" with Sophie. (Hey! That would be my title: "Selfies with Sophie." Kinda catchy, right?) It took me hours, but the efforts was worth it! Almost immediately after I published it, the comments started pouring in on Instagram and Twitter.

"So jealous! Where do I get my hands on one of those?"

"Must. Have. This. Fierce. Bag."

"I LOVE LOVE LOVE this!"

It was fun to see everyone else geeking out over the bag. Keeping up with all of the comments was almost as time-consuming as doing the actual blog post! I definitely owed

Sophie one; this was going to get me a lot more followers and readers. By the time I made it to Delaney's that night, I was practically floating. All my hard work was starting to pay off — I felt like a "Magstar," indeed.

chapter Eight

But over at Delaney's, it became clear that the cloud from yesterday was still hanging over us. Maren, Delaney, and Willow were around Delaney's kitchen table playing a game of Uno, and I kind of stood there awkwardly waiting for them to start a new round so I could jump in. It was like they didn't even notice me, which was even worse than fighting.

"Sorry I'm late, guys!" I said, trying to keep things light and cheerful. "I spent all afternoon working on Magstar. Now I'm really, really ready for a raspberry fizz and some time with my besties."

"Yeah, we were looking at your posts before you got here," said Maren, continuing to play the game instead of turning around to face me. "Seems like you and Sophie had a blast doing all those selfies. With all that black, you're starting to look like her mini-me."

I looked down at my black tank top, chunky black necklace, and dark jeans, one of my "looks" from the shoot. I guess Sophie's style *was* rubbing off on me. But was that a bad thing? She came from LA, one of the world's style capitals. I totally trusted her taste and was always up to play with my own image. After all, what style blogger isn't open to trying new trends and looks?

Now didn't seem like the right time to defend Sophie or tell them about her sleepover invite. I'd try to smooth things over a bit first, which wasn't going to be easy.

Willow patted the seat next to her. "Come sit here, Ash," she said. "We're just about to start a game of Bananagrams, anyway." She started cleaning up the cards that were strewn all over the table.

Oooh! Bananagrams was one of my all-time faves. And apparently, Delaney's younger sister Gigi agreed, because she magically appeared from the living room. (Eavesdropping was one of her specialties, which annoyed Delaney to no end.)

"C'mon, be a good sister and let me play with you guys," she said, tugging on Delaney's cardigan. She turned to Willow, her eyes bright. "Last time, I spelled out 'conundrum,'" she bragged proudly.

"You know the rule," said Delaney, shaking her head 'no.' "No little sisters allowed at sleepovers." Gigi crossed her arms, pouting.

"Aw, let her play," I urged Delaney. I always had a soft spot for sweet Gigi, and Delaney hardly ever let her tag along with us despite her best efforts. She tried so hard! "It's more fun with more people, anyway."

Delaney faced me, annoyed. "Yeah, we all know how you love letting new people barge in — even if they were never invited," she said rudely.

This was starting to get out of hand. Were we only supposed to hang out just the four of us forever? Since when was it against the rules to make a new friend?

"So sue me for not staying in our little bubble all the time," I said, frustrated. "Maybe you should follow my lead and try giving her a chance."

"Why should we?" asked Maren, jumping in. "All she ever does is talk about her fabulous LA life and how she's so much cooler than us. Oh, and let's not forget that her dad is some hot-shot music producer. She seems to think she's above everybody else, and it doesn't help that you think that too!"

Red-faced, Willow tried to break up the tension. "Guys, let's all take a deep breath," she urged. "You know Ashley will always be one of the Sleepover Girls. It's okay if she hangs out with other people sometimes and tries out new looks. It's not that big of a deal."

Still a little shaken, I shot her a grateful look. "Thanks, Wills, for being a voice of reason," I said. It was clearly up to me to set the tone for a fun night and let them know I was still the same 'ol Ashley.

"She's right: I'm a Sleepover Girl first, foremost, and always. Now can we *please* get this party started? I'm ready for some Bananagram action."

Delaney and Maren seemed to chill out a bit, and Delaney dumped the tiles out of the bag onto the table. We all went to work spelling out our words furiously, and Willow was the first to yell, "Peel!" That meant we were all supposed to grab another letter.

After a few more minutes, Maren yelled "Bananas!" which meant that she'd won the round. We all started laughing because she sang the word in an Oprah-style sing-songy voice. But looking at the words she'd made with her letters, my heart sunk. Maren had spelled out "B-A-C-K-S-T-A-B" and she'd built the word "A-S-H" on top of it with one of the "A" letters. She looked me in the eye defiantly.

Delaney looked at it and giggled. "Oh, snap!" she said. "But wait, you forgot something." She took a few of her own letters and built the word

"S-O-P-H" using the letter "S" in "backstab." Feeling hot tears spring to my eyes, I pushed my chair away from the table and ran out of the room onto Delaney's patio porch.

I felt truly awful. My friends were *never* this mean. Did being friends with Sophie mean I couldn't be friends with them? The tears kept rolling down my face. I had never felt unwelcome at one of our sleepovers before. I sat down on the stoop and buried my face in my hands.

I heard the screen door open and soon felt a hand on my shoulder. "It's okay, Ashley," said Gigi, sitting down next to me. "Delaney can be mean sometimes. Believe me, I should know."

I gave Gigi a small smile. That girl might be younger than us, but she sure didn't act like it. I never understood why Delaney was always so annoyed with her. She meant well and was so sweet.

"She's right. They were being totally mean," came Willow's voice from the doorway. "I'm sorry they went off on you. Will a Raspberry Fizz make it better?"

She sat down on the other side of me and tried to hand me the slushie, but I kept my face buried in my hands. I'd lost my appetite. "I just want to go home," I mumbled, still feeling really upset.

"Come watch *Alice in Wonderland*. We can smooth things over, I promise," Willow urged me.

That seemed unlikely. I'd never seen Delaney and Maren act like that to anyone before, let alone me. They obviously needed time to cool down, and I needed to get away from the negativity.

"Sorry, Wills," I told her sadly. "This sleepover is dunzo as far as I'm concerned. Can you grab my sleeping bag? I'm going to call my mom and wait for her out front. I can't go back inside and face Maren and Delaney right now."

As I said the words, I realized that no one had ever left early in our long history of slumber parties. But this one felt *anything* like a party, and who wants to be the odd one out? Definitely not this girl.

chapter Nine

All weekend, I had a major case of the mopes. My mom tried to pep me up by cooking her famous pasta (my fave), and my brothers tried to lure me into a kickball game, but nothing worked. I was still miserable about my falling-out with my friends, and that didn't change when it was time to return to school Monday.

As I put on the faded black jumper Sophie had suggested for school, it actually *felt* like the look fit for once. It totally reflected my mood.

I was feeling so low that I decided to stay under the radar and avoid *everyone,* including Sophie. I didn't want to deal with facing the Sleepover Girls, and I didn't really have the energy to keep up with Sophie today. So, at lunch, I just stayed in the library and curled up in the stacks with a copy of *Pride and Prejudice.* (Now, Jane Austen knew fashion! How I wished petticoats were still a "thing.")

As the day went on, I realized that you never really know how entwined you and your friends are until everything comes undone. It felt so weird to sit on opposite ends of the room from Delaney in study hall, and for Maren and I to pretend we didn't see each other out in the parking lot. At play practice, I could hear them laughing and joking around as I busied myself in the wardrobe closet. *Ugh*. Was it time to go home yet?

I was holed up in the library again the next day when I heard a familiar voice echo through the stacks. "Paging Ashley Maggio, paging Ashley Maggio," called Maren. "Your friends have a very important message for you."

I froze. Had they had a change of heart? Delaney, Maren, and Willow appeared around the corner, smiling at the sight of me on the bean bag chair. "We formed a search party to find our favorite lunch buddy," said Delaney. "Lunchtime isn't the same without you . . . and neither are sleepovers."

I didn't know what to say. I didn't really appreciate the way they'd treated me. But before I could respond, Maren continued, "We totally overreacted. I was taking out my disappointment over the play on you and that is so not cool."

"Yeah, and neither is judging someone we don't know that well," said Delaney. "We'll try to be better about accepting Sophie."

I managed a thin smile for what felt like the first time in days. Life didn't feel right without the Sleepover Girls being in sync. "Promise?" I said. They all nodded eagerly. "That's all I ask."

"We swear on a pile of *Teen Vogues*," said Maren somberly.

I decided to put their promise to the test. "Well, I do have an opportunity for all of us to start over fresh," I told them. "Will you come to a sleepover at Sophie's this weekend? She wants to get to know you guys, too."

Delaney and Maren looked at each other, and then me. "Sure, why not?" said Delaney. "From now on, any friend of yours is a friend of ours."

Now I smiled for real. Even though they'd hurt my feelings, I could understand why the girls felt weird about letting someone else into our circle or the idea of someone "stealing" me away. After all, the four of us had been a tight-knit team for so long! And it must have been weird looking at all those photos of me and Sophie.

Things really did get start to get better after that. I convinced Sophie to sit with us again at lunch the next day, and it seemed like everyone was willing to start over. Sophie kept us all laughing with her stories about playing Barbies with Shira Clay as a kid, and she seemed interested in hearing about Delaney's adventures at the animal shelter, Willow's life as a twin, and Maren's travels around the world with her mom. It felt awesome to see everyone getting along so well . . . finally.

The fun continued at play practice. Willow and Delaney were busy painting teacups, while I was helping do wardrobe fittings backstage. I waved over to them to say "hi," and Willow pointed over to the wings with a smile. Following her gaze, I looked over and saw Maren and Sophie rehearsing lines together. It seemed we were on track for a happy ending.

But, like any great play or story, there's always a snag before the final act, and this would be no exception. On Friday night, Delaney's mom picked up me, Maren, and Willow up for Sophie's sleepover. This was something totally new for us; I couldn't remember the last time we'd been to a sleepover somewhere other than one of our four houses!

When we got there, it was way different than I had pictured. Sophie's family had bought a house in the more rural section of Valley View, with lots of land and plenty of room between houses. It was set in the woods and had a little creek in the backyard. It was super-pretty, but not exactly the glamorous glass mansion I'd pictured.

"Call me if you need *anything*," said Delaney's mom, as we all piled out of the car with our sleeping bags. "I'm just a phone call away."

Delaney rolled her eyes affectionately. "Yes, Mom, we know," she said, giving her a kiss on the cheek. "I'll see you tomorrow. And tell Gigi not to use my flat iron — or anything else in my room!"

Sophie stood at the door, waiting for us. "Come on in!" she invited us. Inside was a bit more along the lines of what I'd imagined — gold and platinum framed records lined the staircase, and the décor looked like a page straight out of a magazine. "Hey," said a girl who must have been Sophie's sister. She was sprawled out on a leopard-print lounger reading.

"Everybody, this is Trina, my sister," said Sophie. "She'll be 'babysitting' us tonight." She used air quotes to show how thrilled she was about that development.

Willow looked uncomfortable. "Oh, your parents aren't here?" she said slowly. She, like all of us, knew we weren't really allowed to have sleepovers without 'rents in the picture.

"It's no biggie," Sophie reassured her. "They went out to dinner in the city . . . some farm-to-table feast or something. They'll be back later."

That seemed like it would probably be okay. Plus, it might be fun to have a girls' night on our own! Sophie led us into the kitchen, where she'd set up a make-your-own s'more station using a fondue pot. "I thought it was the next best thing since my dad isn't here to fire up the fire pit in back," she said, sticking a marshmallow on a skewer and dipping it in the chocolate.

"Just because we can't make 'em outside doesn't mean we can't eat 'em outside," said Maren, staring in awe out the screen door. "Check out that amazing star display!"

Delaney and Willow and I crowded around her to check it out, oohing and aahing at how clear the sky was and all of the cool constellations you could see. After loading up our skewers full of S'more stuff, we all headed outside to get a better look. It really was breathtaking. "There's Cassiopeia!" exclaimed Delaney. "It's the one that looks like a 'W.'"

"Isn't that one named after the vain goddess who couldn't stop talking about how beautiful she was?" asked Willow.

Maren snorted. "In that case, it would be called Franny or Zoey," she joked, and we all giggled. Even Sophie, who, after a few lunches with the Prickly Pair, now knew *exactly* how they'd earned that nickname.

"Speaking of getting gorgeous, I have another surprise for you guys," said Sophie. "Follow me upstairs." I wondered what she had up her silk sleeve this time.

chapter Ten

Curiously excited, we dutifully followed her to her bedroom, which turned out to be very Sophie-esque. The walls were painted with black and white stripes, and her canopy bed was covered in a hot pink comforter, providing a great pop of color. Looking around, I could see Sophie had gone all-out setting up DIY spa treatments. Not only had she set up little areas where we could do facials, manis, and pedis, but she'd also put out fuzzy slippers for each of us on the bed. She had really gone above and beyond to make this sleepover perfect.

I flopped onto the bed to slip on the oh-so-soft slippers. "My toes thank you," I said, cuddling up with one of her satin pillows. This was heaven!

"Oooh, I call dibs on the chocolate face mask!" exclaimed Maren, plopping down on Sophie's vanity stool. Sophie grinned and sat down with Maren to help her get started.

"What's this?" asked Delaney, picking up a jar with some brown stuff inside. She stuck her nose inside and gave it a good sniff. "Mmmm! This smells amazing!"

"Oh, that's a brown sugar scrub I made," answered Sophie. "If you wash your hands and rub it around, it'll make your skin nice and soft."

Delaney gave it another whiff. "You made this? That's amazing! I have to try it," she said, disappearing into Sophie's bathroom. Seeing the open nail station, I set to work giving Willow a French manicure — one of my specialties! The R&R was just what we'd all needed after a stressful few weeks.

After we'd been spa-ing it up for a bit, Trina came to check on us. "Not bad," she said, nodding in approval at Willow's finished French mani. "If you guys are doing the whole DIY thing, you *have* to try this cool hair highlighter pen," she suggested. "My friend's mom works at a salon. She gave it to me to try."

Sophie grabbed the pen from her, looking over the label. "Auburn Vixen," she read out loud. "Ash, this would look *so* good in your dark hair. Be my guinea pig?"

"You should totally try it," echoed Trina. "It'll come out after a couple washes."

I knew my mom wouldn't be thrilled, but if it was cool, it was worth some extra chores. I'm always up for trying something new, especially if it has to do with fashion.

"Sure, why not?" I said, taking Maren's former spot on the stool. Everyone gathered around as Sophie and Trina worked their magic, drawing highlights into my hair. Once they were done, I could see from the looks on everyone's faces that it wasn't quite right.

"Hmm, it's a little gunky and chunky, but I'm sure it'll be fine once you comb it out," said Trina, giving me the once-over.

Seeing the look of horror on Willow's face, I sprang up from the seat to go look in the mirror. Now I could see for myself how ridiculous I looked. The "auburn" highlights looked more like something an orange highlighter had drawn! I was frustrated, annoyed, sad, and mad all at the same time.

Maren knocked on the door. "Can I come in?" she asked, quietly closing the door behind her. Taking one look at me, her face fell. She tried to hide it to make me feel better, but it was hard to miss. "I'm guessing that's *not* the look you were going for."

"You and Delaney were right this whole time," I said, frustrated. "I've been so desperate to copy Sophie and look cool, and now I look like a clown."

"Okay, slow down, sista," said Maren, handing me a Kleenex. "Like Trina said, it'll come out in a few washes. I'm sure you can make it fade enough where it'll be fine before school on Monday. Take some deep breaths, girl."

I shook my head, feeling like an emotional mess. "That's not the only thing," I said, although it was certainly tops on the list. "It's just that . . . I *like* to wear color. I *don't* want to wear black all the time."

"Who said you have to wear black to be cool?" Maren asked. "And since when did you try to copy some else's fashion style?"

"I kind of fell under Sophie's style spell, and now I'm realizing that maybe it's time for me to reclaim my own look. Believe it or not — I actually *hate* that ballerina skirt!" I hadn't realized it 'til I said it out loud, and I felt a lot better right away.

Sophie appeared at the doorway, followed by Delaney and Willow. I could tell by her face that she'd heard everything I said, and I almost started crying again.

"Well, why didn't you just say something? I wouldn't have bought it for you if you didn't like it," she said.

"I know," I said, but Sophie wasn't quite finished yet.

"You're acting like I forced you to overhaul your look. Totally not the case," she said.

I felt like a giant brat. She was right. I'd been her willing copycat. She hadn't done anything wrong. She was just being herself, and I had no right to blame her for anything. It was time for me to apologize.

"I'm sorry, Soph," I said. "I guess I was so excited to have a glamorous new friend, and I wanted to be chic like you. But the truth is, I kind of think black is boring. I need color in my life, and I am going to bring it back!"

"Black is my thing, but colorful is cool and chic, too," said Sophie.

"Not *this* colorful," I said, holding up a lock of my orange hair. And suddenly, everything seemed hilarious. I burst out into uncontrollable laughter, which proved contagious. Pretty soon, we were all sitting on the bathroom floor, holding our stomachs in stitches.

"Oh my gosh!" said Willow. "I haven't laughed that hard in forever!"

Once we'd calmed down, Sophie's face turned serious. "Since we're suddenly taking truth serum, I have a confession to make, too," she said. "The reason we moved to Valley View was that my dad actually got fired from his job in LA. He and my mom decided to start over in a slower-paced city. Hence, here I am . . . on the farm."

I was a little confused. "So he's not really starting a new record label in Portland?" I asked. This explained why sometimes her stories didn't add up, like the maxed-out debit card and her dad supposedly signing Luke Lewis.

"Nope, he's totally out of the industry for good," said Sophie. "I guess I just felt like I needed to pretend the opposite in order to make friends. Back in LA, it seemed like all anyone cared about was who designed my shoes or which superstars my dad recorded with. It's pretty obvious nobody cares about that stuff around here, which is such a relief. I miss LA a little, but I could get used to this life."

"My turn to be honest," said Delaney. "I guess that's why I didn't like you at first. I thought *you* only cared about stuff like that, and it seemed so fake to me."

Sophie shrugged. "I'm not gonna lie. I *love* fashion and the whole Hollywood scene, but that's all I've known my whole life. And as much as I resisted it at first, it's starting to feel like a breath of fresh air to be here."

"Speak for yourself," said Trina, leaning against the doorway. "I really miss LA. I haven't been as lucky as Sophie to make all these new friends yet."

"Well, at least you have your horse," said Willow, trying to reassure her. "I'd love to meet her sometime!"

"What are you talking about? I don't have a horse," Trina said.

Sophie looked sheepish. "Oh, um, yeah. Trina actually *works* at the stables. My dad said she needed to get a job to help out," she admitted. "I kind of fudged the truth on that one, too."

It was weird. We almost always played Share or Dare (our version of Truth or Dare) at our sleepovers. But this felt like a totally new kind of truth game, and it felt really good to lay it all on the table.

"Can we make a pact?" I asked, and everyone nodded. "No more fights. No more lying. No more funeral-colored fashion. And no more hair dye!"

"I'm in," said Sophie. She popped the cap off the highlighter pen and drew an orange streak in her hair. Delaney grinned, grabbed the pen, and did the same, followed by Willow and Maren.

"Good thing I have a top hat to cover this up, even if I am only the understudy," joked Maren.

I felt a huge surge of affection rush through me as I looked around at my friends. "Well, you're all stars in my book," I told them. And I couldn't have scripted this happy ending any better.

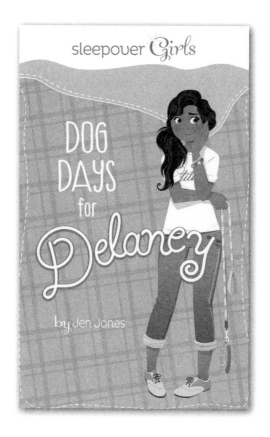

Can't get enough Sleepover Girls?
Check out the first chapter of

Dog Days for Delaney

chapter One

I'm ready to shop pretty much *any* day of the week. I mean, what girl wouldn't be? But Saturdays at the mall are the absolute best. There's live music in the courtyard, good sales, and tons of people are wandering around (which makes for prime people-watching time). My BFFs Ashley, Maren, and Willow always have *tons* of good stories from our people-watching time together.

For as long as I could remember, Maren, Ashley, Willow, and I had been taking turns hosting sleepovers on Friday nights. The tradition had actually started kind of by accident, thanks to me and Maren.

See, Maren's mom works for a travel magazine. She goes on all kinds of cool trips. (Seriously, she's been everywhere — from Switzerland to South Carolina.) Because our moms are friends, my mom offered to watch Maren on shorter weekend trips so she wouldn't miss out on anything. Maren's parents are divorced, and her dad lives pretty far away. She stays with him when her mom was off globe trotting for longer periods of time.

One weekend, Maren invited me to sleep over to return the favor. Her mom said we could each invite one more person. I invited Ashley, Maren invited Willow, and the Sleepover Girls were born! We've been rotating houses ever since, and it's *always* an adventure. I really can't imagine my life without my Sleepover Girls!

Anyway, back to the *real* reason I'm addicted to Sunday shopping. Every Sunday the local animal shelter has its pet adoptions in the parking lot. Every week, they bring a bunch of dogs and cats that need homes. It's so much fun petting and playing with the animals. I guess it's the second-best thing to actually *having* a dog, which I'm determined to do someday. Sadly, I have yet to convince my parents of this, no matter how hard I try.

"You guys, I'm obsessed with this dress," said Ashley. She twirled out of the dressing room wearing a purple print maxi dress. "It was meant to be mine, right?"

Willow picked at the price tag. Her eyes got wide. "Um, more like meant to be a millionaire's! This thing is, like, $350," she said. "I bet I could find some fabric at the store and make you something just as cool." Willow was crazy-artsy. It seemed like there was nothing she couldn't do with a paintbrush or pair of scissors in hand — including sewing.

Ash looked in the mirror, smoothing the sides of the dress wistfully. "I might take you up on that," she said. "Can we at least take a pic for the blog?"

I whipped out my phone to snap a pic, and chose a cool filter effect to make the colors pop even more. "Consider yourself Instagrammed," I told her.

Ashley had just started a Tumblr page centered around fashion called "Magstar." (Her last name is Maggio.) Her blog had actually gotten a pretty good following so far. I wondered how many "likes" and reblogs this one would get. Maybe Ash would even give me a shout-out for shooting the photo. I could see the hashtag now: *#laneybehindthelens*

Clearly bored, Maren grabbed an over-the-top fake fur coat from a nearby rack. "What about this one?" she said, pursing her lips to make a duck face, or as a I call it, the "selfie" face. "Am I top-model material or what?"

The idea of Maren modeling was pretty much unthinkable. She rarely strayed from her "uniform" of hoodie, jeans, and some sort of sports T-shirt. Today it was a Cleveland Browns tank top, which looked adorably ridiculous under the fur coat.

"Okay, that's it," I said. "Maren's going crazy, and I think we're officially over shopping for clothes. Can we *please* go see the dogs now?" Willow nodded in excitement, and I knew Ashley would be game. She was a big dog lover, too, and even had one herself. (Lucky girl!) So once Ashley got changed and reluctantly let go of her latest fashion find, we headed outside to check out the dog adoption.

"Sunlight!" joked Maren, shielding her eyes from the bright light. "Ashley was in the dressing room for so long I forgot what daylight looked like."

Ash took pity and handed Maren her oversized sunglasses. "Here," she said. "You need them more than I do." Maren wearing Ashley's glam sunglasses with her sporty tank top looked totally out of place, and we all dissolved into fits of laughter again.

We finally made it out to the parking lot, where pets and people were gathered under some shady trees. A large banner read "Valley View Pet Rescue." About fifteen dogs were playing and hanging out inside a really big, round open cage. My heart immediately melted, which happens every time I see dogs from the shelter.

"Oh look!" said Willow, pointing at a sweet-looking yellow Labrador retriever. "Delaney, meet my new best friend." I could see why she'd noticed him right away. He seemed to be smiling, with his tongue hanging out. His floppy ears were so precious!

"He *is* a lovebug, isn't he?" Maren said as she petted his head gently. He began nuzzling her arm. Labs definitely seemed to be one of the gentlest breeds. He would clearly make a good companion.

"Oh my goodness! Look at this little muffin," said Ashley, running over to say hi to a fluffy white Maltese with a pink bow in its fur.

"You already *have* a purse dog," teased Maren. Ashley's dog Coco (who was named after famous designer Coco Chanel) was a pint-sized chihuahua who often traveled with Ash in her purse. I blamed it on her reading too many celebrity gossip magazines. Ash loved following in the fashionable footsteps of her fave starlets, all of whom seemed to love parading their pets in the pages of *Teen Vogue*. At least those pets had homes, even if they were treated as accessories.

Ashley petted her huge yellow handbag with a grin. "I always have room for more," she laughed. "Better yet, I could buy another purse!" We all laughed at that.

Ashley leaned over the cage to pick up the fluffball. "Aren't *you* a cutie?" she cooed, rubbing her nose against the dog's. "You'd love to be my purse pal, wouldn't you? Oh yes, you would . . ."

Growl! The dog snapped at Ashley, showing its teeth and hissing. One of the older volunteers rushed over to us and grabbed the dog from a scared Ashley's clutches.

"You should never pick up a dog without asking!" she scolded. She started petting the dog to try to calm it down and quickly walked away.

Then it happened. I saw *my* dream dog. Sitting quietly in the corner, he looked like a mini version of Lassie. A little boy was petting him, and he was just sitting there patiently. He was the sweetest thing ever! As far as I was concerned, it was definitely love at first sight. Now I just had to figure out how to make him mine.

Which friendship-style suits you – Delaney, Maren, Willow, or Ashley?

1. What is your favorite color?
   a) red
   b) yellow
   c) blue
   d) purple

2. Which word best describes you?
   a) loyal
   b) smart
   c) supportive
   d) accepting

3. If a new girl moves to town, what do you do?
   a) ignore her
   b) introduce yourself
   c) smile politely
   d) invite her over

4. If your friend is feeling down, how do you cheer her up?
   a) do something active, like hiking
   b) movie date
   c) craft time
   d) shopping

5. How do you relieve stress?
   a) go for a run
   b) cry a little and then pull it together
   c) focus, focus, focus
   d) write in a journal

6. You get to pick the next event for everyone. What do you choose?
    a) sporting event
    b) dog show
    c) craft show
    d) fashion show

7. Your friend has done something you don't like, you:
    a) ignore them
    b) tell them
    c) let it go
    d) ask them why

8. Your one fault as a friend is that you:
    a) are stubborn
    b) aren't always around when needed
    c) are too quiet
    d) don't always listen

9. Which traits do you like most in a friend?
    a) funny, loyal, and adventurous
    b) low maintenance, generous, and kind
    c) supportive, quiet, and mellow
    d) outgoing, dramatic, and funny

Got mostly "a" answers? You are fiercely loyal to your friends, just like Maren.

Got mostly "b" answers? Like Delaney, your friendship style is generous and kind.

Got mostly "c" answers? You are supportive and a great listener, just like Willow.

Got mostly "d" answers? Like Ashley, you bring the fun and accept everyone.

Want to throw a sleepover party your friends will never forget?

Let the Sleepover Girls help!
The Sleepover Girls Craft titles
are filled with easy recipes, crafts,
and other how-tos combined with
step-by-step instructions and colorful
photos that will help you throw the
best sleepover party ever! Grab all
four of the Sleepover Girls Craft titles
before your next party so you can create
unforgettable memories.

sleepover Girls crafts

Awesome RECIPES
You Can Make and Share

by Mari Bolte

sleepover Girls crafts

Colorful CREATIONS
You Can Make and Share

by Mari Bolte

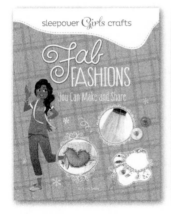

sleepover Girls crafts

Fab FASHIONS
You Can Make and Share

by Mari Bolte

sleepover Girls crafts

Spa PROJECTS
You Can Make and Share

by Mari Bolte

About the Author
Jen Jones

Using her past experience as a
writer for E! Online, Jen Jones has
written more than forty books about
celebrities, crafting, cheerleading,
fashion, and just about any other
obsession a girl in middle school
could have — including her popular
Team Cheer! series for Capstone.
Jen lives in Los Angeles.